THE HOME OF LIGHT

THE HOME OF LIGHT

DEJAN STOJANOVIĆ

Translated by
Željko Mitić

New Avenue Books

&

ALBATROS PLUS

New Avenue Books
&
Albatros Plus

First Edition in English

Library of Congress Control Number: 2024950411

ISBN-13: 979-8-9919466-3-6

THEY SAID ABOUT *THE WORLD IN NOWHERENESS*

"When I got my hands on Dejan Stojanović's book *The World in Nowhereness*, I was amazed and read the book with great pleasure. I did not even believe there was someone today who could write such a long poem, an epic, as if I opened to read the *Iliad* in our time. I recommend this book to all believers in poetry because faith in poetry is the same as faith in eternity and eternal life."

— *Matija Bećković*

"*The World in Nowhereness* is Dejan Stojanović's utopian absolute book, a Mallarméan absolute. An absolute story, or an absolute book, according to Borges, is a desert-like book: sandy, grainily unforeseeable, and corpuscularly innumerable. It is simultaneously a vision and a chimera. Isn't that precisely why we long for an absolute book? *The World in Nowhereness* by Dejan Stojanović is, in his way, an embodiment of that dream."

— *Srba Ignjatović*

"I have always wondered, even about my poetic work, what a total poem is... Can the pentalogy by Dejan Stojanović be called a total poem that every poet of note has dreamed about since Homer? I felt such impulses while reading *The World in Nowhereness*. This is an absolute poem, of an absolute system of thought that reaches across the totality of our civilizational legacies."

— *Duško Novaković*

"Exactly 17 years ago, in the last year of the 20th century, I came across the work of Dejan Stojanović, and then I wrote a text from which I will extract a few sentences. "Dejan Stojanović, in the last two years, made a real feat; he published six books, except for one, all books of poetry." This first five-book collection was published in the last year of the 20th century, and here we are now with the five-book collection in the XXI century, nearing the end of the second decade. And then I also wrote the following: "Stojanović is a poet who searches for the perfect poetic form because at the same time he searches for the absolute meaning of human existence." Whether it was a hunch or not, there is the Pentalogy, and there is that word, that concept – an absolute, an absolute book, an absolute poem that could be sensed even in that first pentalogy, in those poems that he published at that time."

— *Aleksandar Petrov* (January 17, 2018)

"(*The World in Nowhereness* offers) the joy of cognition due to discoveries worthy of the Nobel Prize…"

— *Milan Lukić*

"*The World in Nowhereness* is primarily the result of great literary ambition and faith in literature. It was not only Kiš who said that literature is created by form and that Sartre's quote should be placed at the entrance to the Association of Serbian Writers that "someone does not become a writer to say certain things, but to say them in a certain way." Dejan Stojanović is one of those who think well about that way and think very sovereignly and broadly. Even in how he approaches the form, we can see the breadth of his education, including the humanities and the natural sciences. However, perhaps more than anything else, he enters into some area of spirituality and, I would even dare say, esoteric. If you read Dejan Stojanović, your life will not be the same – it will be better."

— *Muharem Bazdulj*

"It has been quite a while since we had, if at all, a poetic pentalogy in Serbian poetry."

— *Dušan Stojković*

Dejan Stojanović's poetic-philosophical book *The World in Nowhereness*, both in form and content, is an original and exceptional literary work and can be considered a rare literary event in Serbian poetry and on the world stage.

— *Nevena Vitošević*

"It is every poet's dream to write a relevant, unique, comprehensive book in which he will properly present all his thoughts and feelings that have appeared in his long conversations with the world. By the *world,* I mean everything manifested and abstract in (a) language, what is named, and what can be named. Dejan Stojanović's extensive pentalogy *The World in Nowhereness* is an attempt at writing such a book. This pentalogy about the world and light is an ambitious endeavor."

— *Bratislav R. Milanović*

"*The World in Nowhereness*, the pentalogy by Dejan Stojanović, is an unusual endeavor in Serbian literature."

— *Nikola Marinković*

"*The World in Nowhereness*, a poetic endeavor by Dejan Stojanović, is an exceptional occurrence in Serbian."

— *Dragan Kolarević*

"There are very few such books in Serbian literature."

— *Ivan Cvetanović*

"(The publishing of *The World in Nowhereness* is) a significant date in contemporary Serbian poetry."

— *Miljurko Vukadinović*

"Steadfast and consistent, with his mapping out of circular trajectories in the realms of poetry and philosophy, and always being something more than the sum of all parts, Dejan Stojanović has proved to be a thinker of continuously inventive thought. He belongs to that creative ilk whose body of work affirms the permanence of the long-established unity of the Mystic and the Magus. On the one hand, he is one of those with extensive knowledge and who, according to Bela Hamvash, are Mystics. Yet, he is also one of the Magi, who also possesses knowledge, but one meant to encourage and reflect the urge to peer into the other, lesser-known or completely unexplored side, which light cannot reach at first glance."

— *David Kecman Dako*

Dejan Stojanović, a sincere devotee of both poetry and philosophy, achieved a real poetic feat in 2017 by publishing an extensive five-volume book titled *The World in Nowhereness*.

— *Aleksandar B. Laković*

"The author is deeply immersed in his attempt to decode the essence of the universe, the meaning of the origin, and the persistence of being therein. He seeks balance and the possibility of introducing harmony into seemingly incompatible, disharmonious phenomena and concepts."

— *Gordana Vlahović*

"Dejan Stojanović offers us *The World in Nowhereness*, his latest book, as a spiritual anthology. This is an ambitious poetic and essayistic project in a predominantly philosophical, dense, and layered pentalogy about humanity as the source and the final destination of all visible and invisible worlds. The manuscript is presented in innovative, avant-garde form. Dejan Stojanović wisely and expertly intertwines poetry and prose, the epic and the lyrical, and the theoretical-critical."

— *Zorica Arsić Mandarić*

"Stojanović's pronounced contemplativeness is what makes him stand out in the contemporary world of the poetic invention as one of the few being in no quandary about the equality of poetry and philosophy and the necessity of their proper understanding, as well as a deeper decoding of the meaning behind words. For that reason, I see his search in the book *The World in Nowhereness* as a quest for the meaning of elemental survival in a time that is alienated, brutally real, and preoccupied with everything and nothing."

— *Vidak Maslovarić*

"Stojanović's poetic, prosaic, and dramatic approach represents, in a unique sense, an array of basic concepts and elements of human existence, its earthly and cosmic destiny. He tackles the subjects of freedom, the Absolute, God, the Devil, chaos, order, truth, the world, etc. The philosophical, the religious, and the poetic make up the basic core in the interpretation and understanding of the ontology of human survival."

— *Jovo Cvjetković*

Contents

THE HOME OF LIGHT

THE HOME OF LIGHT

Darkness above the sky
A ray in the sky
Life from the air

From the darkness
A firefly shines in the sky –
A ray of darkness

Life shines from space
Whispering the story of the ray.
The home of light is darkness.

HOPE AND MEMORY

HOPE AND MEMORY

Is it possible to lock the World
To prevent it from running all the time

To place it between
Two memories

But what to do in a locked world
To be trapped between the beginning and the end

To count memories
Between the first and the last one

Or live locked up
Inside the memories

Forgotten memories are not dead
They offer an opportunity to hope

In a locked world
We are locked

A world without an end is without hope
An endless hope preserves the memory

It opens the world
And greets it in the space of memories

BE LIGHT

Say light
And be light.
Illuminate while being illuminated.

Say fire
And be fire.
Burn while being burned.

Say water
And be water.
Sail while being sailed.

Say air
And be air.
Inhale while being inhaled.

Say earth
And be earth
While being earth-fed.

Say truth
And be the truth.
Live while being lived.

Say love
And be love.
Love, whether loved or unloved.

Say no to the days that lull you to sleep,
And be a day
Unique.

THE LAND IN WHICH LILIES DON'T DIE

Head over to the land where lilies don't die
And if they tell you to stop
Don't do it
Go, go, just go
And if they call you or wave at you
Don't mind them, just go
Head over toward the land
Where no glance, sound, word, or gesture
Conceals a trap
And if they tell you you're on the wrong track
You just go
And don't look back
Unfortunately for those who remain in sad lands
You can't help them
They can help you even less
And if they tell you, you're a madman or a dreamer
You just fly, fly
Disregard the shouts, the obstacles
Disregard the chronic diseases
Only a strong flight can heal
Fly far away
Do not stop
And if they ask you where you are heading
Just tell them:

Someplace very close

A MOMENT

Inhale this moment
This day and this night

This Sun
And this sky

Let the wind
Confide its secret to you

Live with all your atoms

A MOMENT IN A BRIGHT CITY

A city made of memories
Ancient streets and glimmering landscapes

You're looking forward to the emerging world –
To the undisturbed stream of light and color

No memory can deceive oblivion
Or uncover the origin of the day

You're hovering over the moment
With which you prolong its life and your own

And the moment is already passing

LIFE AND DREAMS IN WORDS

It is not the life that is sad
But the words that interpret it

Life dies in dreamless words
And grows in dreams between words

Unexpressed pain is not less strong
Nor is a happy word less healing than a sad one

Words that speak from dreams do not cry but encourage
Even when they talk about sad things

RETURN

Pigeons nibble on crumbs on the square
Girls flutter like doves
Several older men feed pigeons
Casting wary glances at the girls
Merging with the crowd and disappearing like days
Which tired eyes escort into oblivion

The same picture, the same pigeons, the same older men,
The same glances of the one who observes
From aside, remembering
The days when he didn't feed pigeons
And with a tired look followed the bustle.
Suddenly, he sees himself young
Mixed with the girls
Disappearing among the many strollers

Lost in his thoughts, enchanted by the scene
He realizes that the night lights are already on
And that it's time to go back home

THE SEA

It breathes with waves patiently,
Seducing and reminding
Of the day slowly setting.

Scattered fireflies light up against the black sky,
Streetlamps listen to the murmur of the passers-by,
The courters on the Budva promenade.

The smell of seafood from Mogren
Mixes with wild scents
Of the sea and the strollers,
By the call of the open sea sinking into sleep.

THE EVENING

"Kick it!" "Pass the ball!"
Children yelling awake me from an afternoon nap,
In an adjacent courtyard, a dog barks,
The children's yells mix with the barking.

A cup of half-finished coffee is on the table,
A pile of papers and books waiting for me
To dive straight into the din of their messages.
We never have enough time.

The last rays peak through the window,
Outlines of the beloved mountain before my eyes –
My old friend and teacher,
Telling a new tale with restless colors.

I go out on the balcony;
There are no more children in the yard,
The dog is no longer barking;
The moon appears in the sky.

Slowly falls the night.

THE HOUSE OF SNOW

A SINNER

He refused to kill a bird learning to fly,
He couldn't save anyone from certain death,
He didn't want to learn anything
Leading to a safe result
That opens a safe and wide path
Toward the nirvana of civic contentment.
With every loss, he became more of a winner,
Although nobody saw or realized that.

MATSUO BASHO

Light a fire
While I'm out making
A snowball

The tea we drink will be sweeter
As we watch the snowball
Through this window of ours

In my house
I am your guest
A house within a house

Tea and the whiteness of the snow
A window that is not closed –
A multiplication of reality

You are the window on my house, my friend
And I'm a homeless man
Who makes houses out of snow

LAZAR PECIREP

Here's what Lazar Pecirep was thinking impaled on the stake:

I am on the stake, but you are in bigger trouble
The stake pierces through me
While an insatiable thirst pierces you
Thirsty, you're drowning in your blood

How great is the pain of the soul
That, although tortured, must live
And dies unbearably slowly
On an invisible stake

You can't beat me
Or kill me,
And you know it well

Give me a cigar now

JULIUS CAESAR

Amicus certus in re incerta cernitur.
He had heard these words often,
In battles and during short breaks;
He had heard not an occasion but a quiet truth
In which unspoken words are smoldering;
He had heard them in the hum of the air,
Recognized on the warriors' vacant faces
The echo of an unspoken message
Of his unshaven beard and uncut hair.
Every comrade had known he would do the same
For each of them, and they would do the same for him,
And he knew they all believed Julius, not the emperor.
He was more than Emperor Caesar –
He had been and remained Julius
In the service of Caesar;
And whenever he had heard these words from within,
Julius, not the emperor, began to grow inside him,
A passion awoke in him
As well as (today quite dated) honor.
On horseback or on the throne,
He knew he was Julius.
Without Julius, a Caesar would only be a Caesar –
An ordinary emperor.

HENRY MILLER

Even when he talks about seedy New York neighborhoods
Or about cities of light lacking the light of the heart
Or about the selfish and cavaliers
Or about Tanizaki and his Hiroko
Or about serious people he would behead
He speaks that way because he knows he won't behead anyone –
Millions of heads falling under the swords of the serious
Because he knows his words about urban decay
Will not make any city less foul
Because he knows he's talking about a single city
The same single-family
Because he knows that sometimes in the heart of a geisha, there is
    more spirit,
Wisdom and compassion than in the heart of a princess
Because he knows that only those who hit rock bottom
Truly understand beauty
Because he knows how many sumptuous landscapes die
In the seductive embrace of luxurious armchairs
Because he knows how big machinery is required
To nourish shy reflections of beauty

GHAZALS

GHAZALS

1

All of the great truths come over slowly
Arranging themselves in statements slowly

As a child, I saw my path in a dream-like vision
Along the way, I discovered signposts slowly

All that is fast is not appreciated enough
Impressions infiltrate thoughts slowly

Only thoughts that spend the night inside of one's head,
Glow and come out slowly

A blessèd peace under a tree, in its cool shade,
Records the days going out slowly

Many grand desires are born during journeys
The paths themselves get to find them slowly

While walking around it, the world penetrates us
The images of the world pass through us slowly

What you know and what you don't is of equal worth
Lives depart into the dark slowly

2

What can we say about the Sun?
Life is a hymn to both God and the Sun.

I'm looking for you in impossible places;
For help in my search, I turn to the Sun.

There is no real truth or real lie;
The real truth hides beneath the Sun.

Everything I dream of – comes to life; what I don't dream of –
    dies.
Every morning, I send a kiss to the Sun.

There are no more charming places than the Balkans and the
    Apennines;
They spread lavishly in the Mediterranean Sun.

Even when I sleep, my alert thoughts shine;
My thoughts are my prayer to the Sun.

My thoughts shine on the path when I get lost in a forest.
Dejan's words owe it all to the Sun.

3

Nothing can ever be gained back.
Think carefully about what you wish to gain back.

There is no change, only the flutter of the world.
Once the world wears itself out, it will go back.

Stop from time to time so you don't stumble;
You will not gain the missed steps back.

Pleasant words are more effective than a balm;
With kind words, you will gain the joy back.

We remember experiences; what we oversleep – dies,
Whereas what is false, with defeat, will come back.

Don't count the days; let the days count you;
Into the night, anyway, you must go back.

4

The miraculous world is by nothingness absorbed;
Thought is by the world absorbed.

There is no straight path on the journey;
The path is by the journey absorbed.

They come smiling, but they leave gloomy –
The ruse is sadly by the darkness absorbed.

It's nice to make love secretly on the beach,
Under the eye of the sea that is by us absorbed.

Without light, there can be no beauty
Or gleams of knowledge by darkness absorbed.

Everything that happens has had to happen,
And, with what didn't happen, is by night absorbed.

A kiss has more relevance than a word because a kiss can heal.
The most beautiful word is a kiss absorbed.

5

I admire your lips –
You pronounce my words with your lips.

I fantasize about small delights
And kisses without words on the lips.

She lights up my day,
And my word shines on my lips.

There is nothing but emotions
As I seek the truth on my lips.

The world is beautiful, yet you are even more;
Without you, the world dies silently on the lips.

I can't translate emotions,
Kisses translate them with the lips.

I see nothing while I kiss –
I find the whole world on my lips.

6

The universe, in a single burst, is born,
And its path along the way is born.

Scientists and artists are not screwballs,
But the world which from their thought is born.

We go, we come, we pass –
Every day, the world is born.

I watch a bud develop –
Admiring a rose that is being born.

Sitting on the balcony, I watch passers-by,
Thinking about those who are still to be born.

Everything has to die,
And all that passes is reborn.

Mistakes are not that important,
Along the way, corrections are born.

There are no great truths –
By a small one, a great truth is born.

Don't let yourself fall,
And if you do, in strength, you will be reborn.

When two souls merge and two bodies fall in love,
A new soul is born.

Looking for reasons for everything,
That is why, at every step, trouble is born.

Where is the birthplace of love?
Only in the heart is true love born.

You cannot cheat time –
As it goes along, time is born.

Consolation hides in words –
That is why Dejan, in these words, is again born.

7

We learn something new on our journeys
About the world looking forward to our journeys.

Picture after picture, impression after impression –
Landscapes turn into a movie on journeys.

When going to the park or paying visits to friends,
Or getting home after work, we are also on journeys.

Whole nations and states, entire continents,
Find themselves on long journeys.

A hundred and fifty million years ago, from the sea,
The Balkans and the Apennines sprang on earthly journeys.

Only the change is permanent;
This is most apparent on journeys.

Thoughts travel, and so do dreams and light –
All things in the world are on journeys.

Even when you have stopped, you travel –
Your atoms are on constant journeys.

Nothing is immovable, nothing limitless;
The illusion of infinity hides in journeys.

Where there is no motion, there is no life –
Life cheats death on journeys.

8

Even when the windows are closed, the world for you is waiting –
You are open to the world – in your senses, it is waiting.

Although many are against imagination, I still daydream –
It's nice to illuminate with meaning the darkness that is waiting.

Numerous images flow through my head –
The head is an infinity, thinking and waiting.

The beautiful custom of walking along the promenade is dying.
On the promenade, a smile is always faithful for somebody
    waiting.

There is a giant sea before your eyes and big waves –
For persistent swimmers, the open sea is waiting.

I watch the people, the sea, the sky –
In everything, thoughts for me are waiting.

We meet carefree and part reluctantly –
We choose meetings; parting chooses us in waiting.

9

I only remember what has been verified –
The path to mystery passes through the verified.

As I sit, the world is dead –
Plunging into the unverified, you earn the verified.

Everything is a paradox, and you are one –
Search yourself through what's been verified.

Truth is not the truth because it is so named.
Either the truth is untrue, or its name has not been verified.

In a moonlit garden, surrounded by the fragrance of summer –
An evening that was by impression verified.

Some things you don't need to verify –
The Sun is correct even if not fully verified.

It's pointless to ask for proof of God –
Heaven is large and beautiful even though it is not verified.

10

All that is possible and all that is not possible
Is a part of the world in which all is possible

There is a way and a way out
Even when something seems not to be possible

There are no boundaries
Except for the thought that nothing else is possible

And when you go forward, and when you go back
Some new ideas are still possible

Impotence is not in impotence
But in the acceptance that nothing else is possible

THE VICTORY OF SILENCE

THE UNSPOKEN

She told me many things,
Many more she held back;
I sought her in unspoken words
And always found her in pauses,
Between the words, between explanations.
Every misunderstanding found a solution
In silence and with a conciliatory look,
In a deserved understanding of silence.

A MISUNDERSTANDING

Light spreads in all directions
Open windows and the heavenly blue
A bouquet on the table is waiting to be delivered

A photo from Florence
Among yellow lilies –
She's smiling in the photo

That little picture becomes a movie screen
I see her in many cities
In dance halls and on beaches

The phone rang
And a mere few words later
The sky darkened

AN IDEA

I didn't really know you,
Despite wanting to get closer to you
You stayed a mystery.

I didn't understand your power
Or where the thought came from,
A word in search of you.

You didn't ask for a description,
The word was looking for you.
Even if you don't exist
The thought of you is alive.

You live even if you don't exist.

YOU ARE A DREAM

I picture you surrounded by angels
In other people's smiles, I recognize yours

Dreaming of you, I find you in fairy tales
In cities made of words and notes

I intercept you at an imaginary crossroads,
Preserve in memory

I follow the trails of celestial bodies
Projecting your outlines

And all the while, in my dream,
You are looking for me

A WORD CANNOT BRIDGE THE VOID

I watch your smiling dreams
Flying like birds

Watching your light gait
And a thirsty mouth looking for you

A word cannot bridge a distance
And thirst is ever near

BEAUTIFUL AND DISTANT

When a word deceives a word, thoughts die
When thoughts deceive emotions, ideas die

I have lived through our past and future
And have seen you in all your forms

You were always beautiful yet distant

TWO SHORES

Two searching shores
Long to merge
Extending their lips

A whole world between them
Divides and confuses them

How can one shore find another
How can it swim the ocean
Without the world leaking out

YOUR EYES

Without light, what is hope
What is ascent without smiles

What does the future hide without the truth
What is my story without your word

What is happiness? What beauty
What is my vision without your vision

A LUMINOUS SOURCE

A whisper from somewhere
A picture of a gleaming visage

A scent from somewhere
A smile of the distance

Wings from somewhere
Lifting me up

The first spark appears from somewhere
Into a luminous spring when I land

A FURIOUS DAY

If you face a furious day with your dream –
You alleviate the rage

As you speak from the dream –
The conversation continues

When a whirlwind nests inside the dream –
A path opens before you

On the path –
Your ray protects you

As long as it shines –
You keep on dreaming

And living

A MEMORY

I can still hear your footsteps,
Recognize your face.
The image does not fade,
Senses warm the memory.

You, still alive
Your breath and voice,
The source of a smile,
A memory stronger than reality.

HEAT

I'm not telling you anything new
Nothing extraordinary or funny
And yet your pupil follows mine as I speak

I promise you nothing
And yet your fingers intertwine with mine

Views open up landscapes
Smiles stir imagination

A new light shines over our path
And offers much more than promises

A NEW PLANET

Give me a pair of wings
And fly with me

Fall with me
And cry instead of me
Dream my dream

Find a new planet
On which you will not have to
Live instead of me

A SMILING SILENCE

A smile
Provoked by a smile

A smiling silence
Between words in love

Meaning inhabits silence
Silence inhabits us

Let's watch from it
And dream in it

THANKS

Everything's here
Yet everything slips away

Water is slipping away
As is sound, air, and scent

Landscapes are slipping away
And so is an untouched beauty

Power is slipping away
With the grace of her gait

Days are slipping away
And so are reflections, wars, whirlwinds

Stories are slipping away
And so are judgments, opinions, debates

Skill is slipping away
Another unsung sunset

Opportunities are slipping away
To take a break from trouble

The light is slipping away
To which we failed to say
Thank You

BEFORE DEPARTURE

To stare
To spread the scents
And to kiss a lot

A BLINK OF EMPTINESS

A BLINK OF EMPTINESS

A missing word –
Dormant memory
A spirit hovering
Above oblivion

A desire to say
A desire to hold back
To describe the visible
And grasp the invisible

The visible radiates from the invisible
Signs, symbols, words
Shine in the floating world

In the blink of emptiness

SIGHT AND UNSIGHT

Do I see by sight
Or do I see unsight

Do I see unsight
An insight into all-sight

Inside unsight
Sight is good

With unsight I set sight right
Sight deceives me

In sight, I'm completely
Insightful inward

Stunned by the light
Of the insight

WHEN I AM SILENT IN MY DREAM

Do I live with my dream
Or live my dream

Do I dream of the truth
Or does it dream of me

Do I walk the world
Or does the world walk me

Am I one
Or an image of innumerability

Am I a deception
Or do I look for one

I long oblivion
But I have no peace

I want to say something
Yet impotence tortures me

Only when silent in my dream
Closer to the beauty I get

HARMONY

A word or a note
A letter or a number
The music of numbers – a coveted harmony

The exact Mozart's note
The exact Doomsday
The exact *Mona Lisa*

Consecrated sages empower words,
Images and notes through numbers

Where there is no number, there is no harmony
Where there is no harmony, a quarrel breaks out

WE SHOULD INHALE THE WORLD

We should inhale the world
Stories lack the power of the air

Winged by sight
We should sink

Decompose both oxygen and hydrogen
Absorb

Inhale clean elements
And fly

A STORY IS JUST A STORY

The strongest arm
The strongest mind
Remain powerless

A story is just a story
A description remains a description

Even if you touch the light
And sense the invisible outlines
You can't tell the secret

ANOTHER WORD

Another flight
Another shout
Smile and look

Another gale
Another flower
The scent of space

One more word –
A deserved path

A SMALL TRUTH

That small truth
That small word

From which a great tale is born
The story grows and is transmitted

Suddenly, everyone forgets about the small truth
The small word

Everyone wants big tales
Great truths

But the tale becomes too big
In danger of dying under its weight

Then someone recalls the small word
Small balmy truths

And, step by step,
Starts to go back

LITTLE AND BIG

A little and a little put together are bigger than a lot at once.
It is too much to ask too much right away.

STRENGTH

You are stronger
You are not
I am stronger
I am not

They are stronger
Who are not
We are stronger
We are not

They've found a way
They've slipped through
They are stronger
They are not

They are laughing
They are bragging
They are strong
They are not

It just seems
So, for a moment
They are only strong
While the deception lasts

HANDS

Down
Down
Way down

Pray
Pray
All-day

Hands
Hands
All alone

LONELINESS

Alone so I wouldn't be alone
Alone even in company

Alone so I could dream
Alone and yet not alone

Alone so I could create
Alone and yet residing in others

Alone so I could live
Alone and yet others reside in me

Alone so that I would be with everyone

GUILT AND VENGEANCE

ARGUMENT

To strive for precision
Passing through the prairie
In which nothing is precise,
Where there is no valid order,
Where uncertainty instills order.

Survival as the only goal,
The power that beautifies,
And the power that makes us ugly –
The beauty of a tiger jump,
And bloodthirstiness as the only possibility.

To struggle for a more precise word,
A more precise hit,
A more precise stab at the victim's body,
And to enjoy the prey
In the perfect trap of the argument.

NOTHINGNESS

How to defeat nothingness
If it is both before and after

Eternity, or the moment of eternity, is waiting
A trap, a whirl, and a flurry

How to outwit the darkness
That has always been there

Which waits before and after
Without returning or leaving

Or is this moment
A source, an exit, and a victory

CONSCIENCE

Accustomed to the nest
Awake as we sleep

It guards and watches
Instead of us

Deceptively turbulent
It defends its nest

It is her goal
That the nest be a nest to itself

WISDOM

Everyone who runs does not reach the finish
Sad, you wonder how come
You're late even though you run
And someone is slow yet arrives on time!

He runs slowly
You rush
He pauses to check
You fly over

He takes breaks
Drinks some water
Ever fresh and calm
You give up

You were so happy
For your speed and luck
And yet he trot-trot-trotted
Way ahead of you

SMALL PLEASURES

The size is confusing
Opportunity awaits in the small

A small truth is bigger than a big scam
Sometimes it is so with people, too

The big ones become small
Small ones become big

A novelty sleeps in a hidden truth
A small opportunity awakes it

A side view provides an opportunity for opportunities
Time rarely makes mistakes

Excessive speed slows down
With a large number of accidents

The angle changes constantly
The distance offers a good view

NATURE

The music of the morning
The Sun sends its regards

A saddled horse drinks spring water
Before darting into the green space

The grass speaks of the earth
The mountain heights have a calming effect

Away from the infectious din
Unhindered solitude

There is no one to disturb the harmony
To pollute the spring water

No one to spoil the view
Solitude is a good company

THE FOREST

Beasts surround you
But many cannot read the forest's alphabet

The forest is your homeland
Although you are unaware of it

Learn to hunt
Peace is an illusion

THE CITY

Unlike the forest, the city is lit even at night
Although the city itself is a rustling forest

Bright cities and forest noises
A light that protects and a noise that instills fear

The city uses its light to drown the forest's muffled noise within
Despite being cheerful, it is no less dangerous than a dark forest

The city is a cloaked forest
And its streets – an illusion of order

POWER

Calm and ascended
You are a heavenly sigh
Intoxicated and intoxicating

Power's powerlessness
A scream from the night
A tender look from the heart of power

Power contrasted by power
Magnificent, yet modest and soft
You shine from the heart of power

DREAM AND REALITY

Is reality what we think it is
Or what it makes of us

Is the dream more real than the day
Or is the day the source of the dream

Is the day worth it without the dream
Or is the dream the source of the day

Is light stronger than darkness
Or without darkness, there can be no light

Is life the truth or the dream
Or life lives us with the dream

IMAGINATION

Imagination is an attempt
To bridge the void
To fly the Universe
In the thought shuttle
Peek into the invisible
Touch the intangible
Materialize dreams
Express the unspeakable
Explain the mystery
Break all boundaries
Turn nothing into something

SERENITY

The distance heals and offers serenity.
Before the distance, we become smaller
And wiser by listening to infinity.

HAPPINESS 2

It has value
Yet, it can't be sold or bought

Formed before banks and factories
Before rockets and computers

Larger than the largest tower
Brighter than the largest lighthouse

Sometimes, it flees from the courts
To spend the night in ratholes

It always seems to be in reach

A FRAUDSTER

He has nowhere to hide
Caught in his own trap

A trap set for another
Captures his misstep

His deception tightens
The noose around his neck

OFFENDER

We talk
Because we don't dare to kill

We last gradually
In anticipation of the outcome

In the meantime
We search for flaws in the victims

Justification for our actions
As we sneak quietly

Rarely does one recognize the game of the executioner and the
    victim
Skill is on the side of the executioner

GUILT AND VENGEANCE

Revenge is never late
Although we forget the guilt

Someone has done wrong once
Or so it just seemed

The reason has been forgotten and resolved
But the guilt and revenge keep on going in circles

It will be that way
As long as there is someone to take revenge on someone else

Until the last human is left alone
With guilt on his hands as his only legacy

A MASQUERADE

You used to like masquerades
As a way to escape from reality

You liked the innocent game of disguise
But you've got tired of it

The masquerade is turning into its opposite
It cannot be a substitute for escape forever

You observe the hiding faces
Seductive smiles

You hear words that don't speak
Each mask becomes a face

The real face is buried and lost deep within
The face masks are mingling on the surface

Nobody recognizes anyone –
The monotonous diversity of the mask

The main stars of the masquerade
Don't even recognize themselves

ICE CUBES

You suffocate
Sobbing inaudibly
Surrounded by ice cubes

Their eyes issued a cry:
"Freeze!
Freeze!"

And if you don't freeze
The sad ice cubes
Ask for comfort and warmth from you

RADIANT FACES

They enunciate big and beautiful words
Paradise is just about to arrive

You look radiantly at their radiant faces
Sunlit for this particular occasion

You listen to their words
Intoxicated by sweet sounds

You wonder where so much goodness comes from
And realize too late that words are cheap

Their story holds your attention
Until the hand of reality pulls you away

Until the numerous faces
Remind you of the light that hasn't come

While someone's ears yearn for words
You cannot tell them

THE DESERT

All the words have spilled out
Spread around long ago
Became alienated

Thoughts are petrified
And the eyes looking for them
In the wasteland

All the words have canceled themselves
And do have all the ideas

THE ECHO

Without other people's sight, I am also blind
A world as its own echo

THE RED DEVIL

The red devil
Revived by the moonlight
Watches from the top of the skyscraper
While the world peacefully sleeps

CITIES

ATHENS

A city, an idea nourished by many other ideas, nourished by air, water, sun, nourished by life, sprouted from the earthly stone, which builds a court from that same stone and raises it despite time, despite the darkness. It rejoices in light as an eternal source and finds light even in the darkness; it erects a radiant temple that defies emptiness, barbaric hordes, ugliness, mud, stupidity, and apathy and only finds meaning in beauty.

The wings of the Nike of Samothrace are flying toward the distant light, carried by the knowledge of its origin from before the earthly creation. They are flying toward the source of the eternal city from which the power that supplies all the magnificent cities springs. The light of Athens is flying into the void, building earthly gardens of hope.

ROME

There are but two eternal cities – the city of God and Rome, which opens a view of the eternal city from the Capitol, sends a prayer from the Palatine and gives birth to a new idea on the Esquiline Hill. At the same time, some miracle always happens on the Quirinal, and some new goddess sees the light on the Viminal Hill, while the Sun halts over the Caelian Hill, and the whole spirit of the Roman squares sets off toward the Aventine Hill. The city of God and the eternal city then merge into one.

Rome – the city of all cities, the idea of all ideas – shines radiantly over the land and the sea. The eternal city – an idea that does not die with a passing day, a passing year, or a century, that does not die with the death of emperors, in the ruins of misunderstandings and deplorable historical gossip, which is stronger than empires, stronger than individuals, which shines from the immortal spirit that even barbarians could not harm, even though, at times, they may even have been a solution; momentarily, until a new resurrection, until a new glory. The barbarians are not persistent and skilled enough to destroy everything for which a day, a year, a century, or centuries would not be sufficient for them to accomplish.

CONSTANTINOPLE

Alive and dead Byzantium – sublimity and pretense. Byzantium springs from a fairy tale, and Constantinople springs from Byzantium's dreams. Just as Rome did once, it feeds the same dream, the same idea: it builds gates on two seas to defend the Eastern and Western empires of a dreamed Europe, a European fairy tale and truth. It is fed by sea air, by atoms powered by greatness for millions of years before its rise. The most mysterious city kept the secret of other cities lost in time; the eyes of other Europeans and the eyes of Turkish horsemen yearned for it. The city of the most beautiful European women and arrogant patrician spirit contained the seeds of decline.

Constantine the Great, the first Christian emperor, could not predict the fate of his city, nor could Justinian change history with his code and the construction of the Hagia Sophia, which elevates the dome of human skill and power toward the universe, toward the mystery from which the very domes rise despite the fragility of all human endeavors. Constantinople is a reflection of Europe – an image of possibilities and an image of danger, encouragement, and warning.

FLORENCE

The first modern city, the first modern culture, a renewal of old ideas, a declaration of war on lethargy, the first modern great spirits, the first Madonnas in paintings outside the churches, the first signatures in them. Merchants and nobles, military leaders and politicians weaving intrigues. Politics is understood as the science of achieving the goal, not the ideals and the success measured by the ideals – more important names in one place than in the whole modern world. Florence puts to shame every modern metropolis. It is the eternal dream of painters, dreamers, and all who live for their dreams.

VENICE

A city of dreams, lovers, and gondoliers. Every Venetian canal carves a story into a dream; every Venetian square remembers an endless tale of seducers and schemers, Jesuits and Franciscans, thinkers and Inquisitors. Venice is a name that would suit the most beautiful woman. It is an elusive female, an elusive fairy and goddess. It is not just a city; it is a dream that proves that the dream is real, that the dream is possible, that reality is what is won by strength, that an idea is a reason to live, and that art is what one unconditionally surrender to, without expectations.

Venice gathers its spirit and visions in St. Mark's Square, sending new dreams toward future Venices. The open sea inspires dreams. The same challenge that drove Marco Polo awaits new sailors to respond to the call of the sea. Venice is not a city built on canals:

> It travels and swims the water
> It is the very water over which it rises
> It is the very dream to which it aspires
> It is a gondolier's song
> It is a lamp
> Reflected in the eternal water of its dream.
> *La Dominante, Serenissima, Venice.*

PARIS

Hemingway came up with the best description – the city of light; Baudelaire saw its other side – the city of the spleen; Balzac described its salons and orphanages – a city of contrasts; in it, Prévert sang about Barbaras from other cities – a city of love and contradiction, of showing the right path and leading astray. French and foreigners equally love it. Picasso is a Frenchman as much as Delacroix and hundreds of thousands of other painters who, toward the end of their lives, cannot remember precisely why they came to this city long ago, feeling hopeful.

Paris is a city of delusions and revelations, revolution and enlightenment, Camus and existential sorrow, boulevards, heavenly fields, tradition, art, merriment, madness, debauchery, kings and clowns, business people and demimonde, Toulouse-Lautrec and prostitutes. Paris is the goal of all artists, the unfulfilled dream of those who fortunately never arrived in it in pursuit of artistic happiness; the realized dream of the unrealized, the misunderstood dream of the understood, the futile dream of arrogant and schizoid chauvinists; a city of libraries and bookshops, and unavoidable cafes; a maze of colors and scents in which colors change color when illuminated by the sunlight of numerous ideas sprouting daily in the minds of all who came to this city with big dreams and meager chances. A city of machines that grind all those ideas and dreams and perseveres despite ideas and dreams, despite the destructive revolutions of those who seized their opportunity to the detriment of the city (or to its benefit), to the detriment of Champs-Élysées, to the detriment of other innocent cities, to the detriment of ideas that had no chance under the destructive blow of imbeciles possessing enormous power.

The city of light lives peacefully amid unrest, as if nothing horrible had ever happened, as if there had never been any revolutions. A city of thinkers, philosophy, and enlightenment; of semi-forgotten Sartre and his "revolutionary" ideas; a city containing other neighborhoods-cities – Latin Quarter, Montparnasse, Pigalle, Montmartre, Boulogne; neighborhoods that hide other cities of streets, streets of secret cities living in parallel in the spleen of the luminous city on boulevards that like rivers flow out of dreams of new conquerors, new minds and fliers longing for a bit of stardust, a little taste of glory in the city of all dreams, an imaginary city, a city to which one aspires but in which one never arrives finally and completely; towards which, despite countless bridges, no bridge has yet been built toward the city's true center. Its center remains out of reach; it changes the center – not the center of the labyrinth, not at the beginning or the end. It is a philosophical circle with an unreachable center from which the city of light sprouts to fly toward the source of light on the wings of its own.

SHAKESPEARIA

Shakespearia is an enormous city – overcrowded; it's as big as London. This city lacks very few things. Everything that makes a city great and important already exists in Shakespearia. In terms of influence, it is more significant than many other cities.

It has its fountains and promenades,
Its Veronas and gardens,
Its kings and Juliets,
It owns the whole of Denmark,
And its prince,
It has a black man in love,
It has its sonnets,
Its summers and days
Which compares to the beauty of young men
Or girls
Its tears and its laughter,
Its mystery and truth,
Its drama
From which it sings about meaning.

MOSCOW

It bathes with snow in the light; it outlives empires and ideas; neither Napoleon, Hitler, Lenin, nor Stalin could conquer it. Where Constantinople sank, Moscow was born, but due to the tectonics of history, it moved a little further away from the sea and the coast and grew in a slightly colder place. Although no one knows or will admit it, Moscow is the new Constantinople, the new center of the Eastern Empire, the new center of the West in the East. Geography is irrelevant here. There are not two Europes – there is only one.

We admire the Russian Cossacks who defend Moscow and Europe. God, who was oblivious of this city for a century, now returns to the Moscow region and rejoices in the high tones of Vysotsky, the ballads of Okudzhava reminding one that Paris was never too far away, that the connection was not accidental, nor was love for the French language; that there is a reason why the French admired Turgenev so.

Questions of honor provoke no more duels, no miraculous natures of Pushkin and Lermontov; new duels arise in oligarchies and criminal enterprises, in the games of the upstart plutocracy, but Moscow went through much bigger turbulences before and survived them all.

BELGRADE

Belgrade was a small Rome that still hides a Rome in itself. The Roman Singidunum – the White City, growing from two rivers – old and a new city, an old and a new idea; until a little over a century ago – a small town.

The idea of the old Belgraders is a rumor – the roots last longer than a mere century. Belgrade is not the most beautiful city, but its vast waters still remember the story of Singidunum and still transmit far and wide the secret that spreads through Knez Mihailova St, Kalemegdan, Ada Ciganlija; they carry the secret that radiates from the faces of its women.

The old spirit and pride shine in a new place.

CETINJE

Due to unfortunate circumstances, it is a capital city situated among mountain peaks near Lovćen, where even God is closer. Seemingly forgotten by the rest of the world, it defended that same world for centuries, preserving what many others had lost – freedom.

A SNOW CITY

A snow city is not a city – it is an idea larger than any city. No city longs for light more than the snow city, and no city is more bathed in whiteness. A great hero is born in this city every year as the snow melts. All these heroes devise a significant undertaking every year. Skill, strength, wisdom, and heroic spirit are the conditions for survival. There are no more agile seamen dreaming of sunlit cityscapes, sailing the seas while being propelled by the eternal fire of the Sun, which they worship from the whiteness of their earthly landscape.

The Vikings – the sons and daughters of the snow city, the sons and daughters of the Sun, fed by the purest elements of their stellar origin, the most beautiful heroes who have ever lived, the most stunning women who still live in Denmark, Sweden, and all of Scandinavia. The Hyperboreans in the new Hyperborea.

NEW AMSTERDAM OR NEW YORK

The Netherlands in New York. The city canyons for which the Flying Dutchman carved the direction initially, while the spring was small. The canyons of streets with no end in sight. *The Asphalt jungle*, the Atlantic megalopolis, a coastal city forest. At the heart of the city is a park.

New York is a multi-citied city. It compresses the whole world between Park Avenue and the Atlantic coast, the lights of Broadway, and the artistic atmosphere of Greenwich Village. It contains an entire city of theaters and a whole city of Metropolitan Opera and Museums. It preserves a magnificent picture of another city – *the View of Toledo* by the Spanish Greek El Greco. In New York, I experienced Toledo, visited Toledo, and realized that

Every big city hides its Toledo within

Its mystique

Its elusive color

Its towers

Rising toward the slightly gloomy-blue height

As if remembering the common origin

New York connects worlds and shores. Spain and Greece also live in New York, right next to England and the Netherlands, right next to the whole world in one magical, noisy, opulent, and hectic place.

CHICAGO
My kind of town

Next to a lake larger than some seas, in a vast plain that perhaps with its distances inspired Hemingway in Oak Park, Sandburg, and Bellow to write; Frank Lloyd Wright and Mies van der Rohe to design the towers of the modern metropolis, to connect the line of the possible with the unattainable.

The city with the largest number of Nobel laureates, one of whom has convinced me that universities are, after all, slums in the mercantile sea. In the Eldorado of Dreams, a city of sports and workers from all sides, hungry for games and achievement of an impossible dream in the promised land.

Every American city hides an Eldorado within; whoever comes to America is looking for an Eldorado. Sometimes, people arrive in Eldorado, which they built. Still, nobody realizes that the Eldorado is a city that lives within us, greets us after our travels and wanderings, warns and directs us. Still, its light fades under the lights of cities that offer something different. The Eldorado remains an unrealized dream, a Garden of Eden, a lost bliss.

Meanwhile, everybody forgets the dream and the Eldorado they used to long for while soaking in a river of realistic dreamers who admire the human achievement on the *Magnificent Mile* of Michigan Avenue, hoping for another mile.

SAN FRANCISCO

A golden city with a golden bridge, a blue city in the bay, a white city on the hills. Rome sits on seven hills; San Francisco undulates on countless. Water and the Sun are in contact with the sources. A dream that sprouts from the water climbs the hills to meet the heights and human intent. A city awakened and raised from a fairy tale – American Constantinople, America in the Mediterranean, the Mediterranean on the coasts of the Pacific Ocean, Europe in America, and America in Europe – an achieved vision – a whole world in one place.

Almost no modern city has a mystery. Despite being modern and new compared to European cities, San Francisco radiates the charm of a mystery hidden by an invisible haze, an invisible corona, in the middle of the air. It appears as if, by some miracle, it had sprung from the sea and moved to the surrounding hills to soar up high.

LOS ANGELES

While walking up Rodeo Drive (Beverly Hills) with my friend Kelly, I think about Budva (Montenegro). We arrive at McCormick & Schmick's restaurant at the top of the street. Pretending to be sitting in *Mogren* (Budva), I glance at the Regent Hotel across the street, across the noisier Wilshire Blvd. below Rodeo Hills. Two older French couples are whispering at an adjacent table, and Kelly compliments them in French. At another table, several people are hollering in the Serbian about the political situation in Serbia and Belgrade.

We leave the restaurant; a tall young man with a boy intercepts us and asks Kelly to take a photo with his little brother. Kelly accepts, but the young guy asks for a photo and a phone number. I think that nothing like this has ever happened to me in Chicago. New surprises and nonsense are still awaiting me in Santa Monica, in boutiques, at gas stations, with all those men who think that Kelly (despite being a model at one of the biggest agencies and an aspiring actress) is a movie star.

A belle in a crazy city. One of many, in a city where you cannot tell people apart in the streets, in a restaurant where a beautiful and unfulfilled actress works, still hopeful for success, at an airport where transportation offers you a screenwriter and director who has a breakthrough idea and hopes that you are the one who will enable its realization.

Los Angeles lives in the suburbs. Hollywood extends over the hills like San Francisco: the dream of all possible artists, actors and directors, the dream of all beautiful women, and those who dream of attractive women. No other city people visit and move into with more dreams and leave with more disappointments; there is no city of grander illusions nor a city that rewards those who have realized their dreams in it with greater glory.

Walking down Sunset Boulevard, I spotted a small sun rising from the big Sun and gliding toward me. It laughed and appeared to murmur some strange words, and then it bounced its way back until it went out on the boulevard's horizon in the twilight of the great setting Sun.

THE NEW CITY

I invite you to a new planet. It is so big that everyone can build their city on it. Some may choose to build a library city; some will build a fairytale city; some will want a city of parks, some a city of science and computers, and some a city of love. This will be the capital city of the New Planet. Romeo – the king, Juliet – the queen. This city will be the Arch of Triumph, the central place where the streets will lead to other cities. Streets leading to the capital will connect all cities.

New Planet Day will be an official Holiday once a year. Everyone will bring something from their cities: books, birds, flowers, spaceships, the latest computers that can think, movies from this and other planets, perhaps even aliens. Everyone will gather around the huge central temple dedicated to the Sun and the World, and every year, they will kindle a big fire, which will new Vestals guard and not have to preserve their virginity, except for the purity of their soul.

When all the cities, streets, and inhabitants come together, it will dawn on everybody that the whole planet is one big city.

A GHAZAL IN FLOWERS

Once a week, pick a flower –
Gift someone with your attention's flower.

People collide and contend –
Sometimes, the solution is a flower.

I did not open the book you sent me,
Yet in it, there was a pretty thought's flower.

The sea, air, and forest is fragrant;
The whole universe is a flower.

When you love, your emotions become fragrant –
Love is a flower.

Both in the depths and the darkness
There is a dormant, bright flower.

Attention is worth more than gifts –
Dejan gives you this flower.

Notes on Ghazals

Ghazal is a poem consisting of couplets – from five to fifteen, usually seven to twelve. Each couplet is independent, like an epigram. A traditional ghazal is also metrically precise regarding metrical feet or syllables. Despite various variations existing in the West, especially in English, in which enjambments are used, this is still unacceptable in the traditional ghazal, the form of which is inviolable. In the conventional ghazal, enjambments can be used neither within a single couplet nor by being transferred into others. There is a logical basis for this, as the second verse brings surprise, resolution, and reversal. Also, one must not deviate from the rule that the first couplet, at the end of both verses, must end with the repetition of the same word or phrase, preceded by rhymes. In each subsequent couplet, but only in the second verse, this word is repeated as a refrain (preceded by a rhyme).

The ghazal originated in Persia in the tenth century. The form arrived in India in the twelfth century.

All the poems in the "Ghazals" cycle were written in this form, as well as the ghazal at the end of the book; the only difference is that the Ghazal number one was the only one that was made in a strictly traditional way, with rhymes and metrical precision, while rhymes were absent in other ghazals.

The pattern:

The first couplet:

-------------------------- rhyme A + Refrain

-------------------------- rhyme A + Refrain

The second couplet, the third, and so on:

-------------------------- rhyme A + Refrain

Notes on the Poems' Creation Dates

The poem "The Red Devil," from the "Guilt and Vengeance" cycle, was written in the early 1980s.

Poems written between 1996 and 1999:

The "Hope and Memory" cycle: "A Moment," "A Moment in a Bright City."

The "The Victory of Silence" cycle: "You Are a Dream".

The "Guilt and Vengeance" cycle: "Nothingness," "Small Pleasures," "Nature," "The Forest," "The City," "Dream and Reality," "Imagination," "Guilt and Vengeance," "A Masquerade."

Poems written between 2000 and 2001:

The "Victory of Silence" cycle: "An Idea" (2001), "A Luminous Source" (May 2001), "A Furious Day" (December 2000), "A Memory" (February 2001), "Heat" (December 2000), "A New Planet " (2000), "A Smiling Silence" (2000), "Thanks" (May 2001), "Before the Departure" (January 2001).

The "A Blink of Emptiness" cycle: "Sight and Unsight" (August 2001), "When I Am Silent In My Dream" (May 2001), "Harmony" (May 2001), "The World Should Be Inhaled" (2001), "A Story Is Just a Story" (May 2001), "Another Word" (February 2001), "A Small Truth" (August 2001), "Little and Big" (May 2001), "Strength" (July 10, 2001), "Hands" (2001).

The "Guilt and Vengeance" cycle: "Conscience" (September 2001), "Wisdom" (September 2001), "Power" (29.12.2001), "Desolation" (July 27th, 2001), "Serenity" (February 2001), "Happiness 2" (July 2001), "Ice Cubes" (2000), "The Offender" (February 2001), "Radiant Faces" (February 2001), "The Echo" (July 2000).

Poems written in 2006:

The "Victory of Silence" cycle: "A Word Cannot Bridge the Void" (January 2006), "Beautiful and Distant" (January 2006), "Two Shores" (January 2006), "Your Eyes" (January 2006).

The "A Blink of Emptiness" cycle: "A Blink of Emptiness" (January 27th, 2006).

The rest of the book was written in 2008, except for the poem "The Land in Which Lilies Don't Die," written on February 23rd, 2009.

The Index of Titles

Guilt and Vengeance,
Hands,
Happiness 2,
Harmony,
Heat,
Henry Miller,
Hope and Memory,
Ice Cubes,
Imagination,
Julius Caesar,
Lazar Pecirep,
Life and Dreams in Words,
Little and Big,
Loneliness,
Los Angeles,
Matsuo Basho,
Moscow,
Nature,
New Amsterdam or New York,
Nothingness,
Offender,
Paris,
Power,
Radiant Faces,
Return,
Rome,
San Francisco,
Serenity,
Shakespearia,
Sight and Unsight,
Small Pleasures,
Strength,
Thanks,
The City,

The Desert,
The Echo,
The Evening,
The Forest,
The Home of Light,
The Land in Which Lilies Don't Die
The New City,
The Red Devil,
The Sea,
The Unspoken,
Two Shores,
Venice,
We Should Inhale the World,
When I'am Silent in My Dream,
Wisdom,
You Are a Dream,
Your Eyes,

The Index of First Lines

A little and a little put together are bigger than a lot at once,
 Imagination is an attempt
The music of morning,
Accustomed to the nest,
Darkness above the sky,
The strongest arm,
You used to like masquerades,
He has nowhere to hide,
It is not life that is sad,
He refused to kill a bird learning to fly,
I didn't really know you,
Nothing ever can be gained back,
I'm not telling you anything new,
A whisper from somewhere,
Beasts surround you,
She told me many things,
Revenge is never late,
A smile,
I only remember what has been verified,
Give me a pair of wings,
We learn something new on our journeys,
Light a fire,
"Shoot!" "Pass the ball!"
Here's what Lazar Pecirep was thinking impaled on the stake,
A word or a note,
A missing word,
Alone so I wouldn't be alone,
Everyone who runs does not reach the finish,
Everything's here,
The Universe, in a single burst, is born,
All the words have spilled out,
Light spreads in all directions,
We should inhale the world,
The miraculous world is by nothingness absorbed,

All that is possible and all that is not possible,
It breathes with waves patiently,
That small truth,
I can still hear your footsteps,
Calm and ascended,
If you face a furious day with your dream,
Inhale this moment,
Head over to the land where lilies don't die,
The red devil,
What can we say about the Sun?

ABOUT THE AUTHOR

Dejan Stojanović was born in Peć in 1959. He graduated from the Law School of the University of Priština. He has published these books of poems:

Circling (Krugovanje), Narodna knjiga – Alfa, Belgrade, three editions – 1993, 1998, and 2000.

The Sun Observes Itself (Sunce sebe gleda), NIP Književna reč, Belgrade, 1999.

The Sign and Its Children (Znak i njegova deca), Prosveta, Belgrade, 2000.

The Creator (Tvoritelj), Narodna knjiga, Belgrade, 2000.

The Shape (Oblik), Gramatik, Podgorica, 2000.

The Dance of Time (Ples vremena), Konras, Belgrade, 2007.

Pentalogy: *The World in Nowherness (Svet u nigdini):*

1. Ozar (Ozar), Udruženje književnika Srbije, Belgrade, 2017.

2. The World and God (Svet i Bog), Udruženje književnika Srbije, Belgrade, 2017.

3. The World in Nowhereness (Svet u nigdini), Udruženje književnika Srbije, 2017.

4. The World and Humans (Svet i ljudi), Udruženje književnika Srbije, Belgrade, 2017.

5. The Home of Light (Dom svetlosti). Udruženje književnika Srbije, Belgrade, 2017.

The Hidden Light (Skrivena svetlost), Čigoja, Belgrade, 2018.

Primordial Spark (Iskra iskona), Albatros plus, Belgrade, 2021.

Centuries and Steps (Vekovi i koraci), Albatros plus, Belgrade, 2023.

Essays:

Creator and Creating (Stvaralac i stvaranje), Albatros plus, Belgrade, 2021.

The New Man and the New World (Novočovek i novosvet), Rad, Belgrade, 2022.

Anthology: *Selected Serbian Plays* (*Izabrane srpske drame*), USA, 2016.

Philosophy: *Absolute*, New Avenue Books, USA, 2024.

A book of his selected interviews, Conversations, was published in 1999 by NIP Književna reč, Belgrade. The Serbian Heritage Foundation and the Association of Writers of Serbia for Intellectual Engagement awarded the book the Rastko Petrović Prize.